IMITATION OF LIFE

IMITATION OF LIFE

L. MARIE WOOD

FALSTAFF
BOOKS
WWW.FALSTAFFBOOKS.COM

Black Dress

The closet is full of her things
from baby clothes
to teenage dreams.

Always some new trend
changing every week
up 'till the very end.

Searching rapidly,
haphazardly,
for the black dress.
Plain-Jane,
fashionless
black dress.

Tears fall like rain drops
on her cheeks
as she pulls,
pushes,
prods,
and peeks.

All the way in the back
just beyond her reach
hangs the black dress
she desperately seeks.

Unchanging,
timeless,
eternal
black dress
for to 'dorn her daughter
at rest.

Four Crosses

Four crosses on the side of the road
white with floral wreaths around their tops,
colors of blue and red and purple and yellow there
waving goodbye.
White so white it glows against the backdrop of brown
soon green
was green
always green but brown now as the soil heals.
Driven and churned
puddles form in the imprints
grass spouts to trace it
pattern it
remember it.
I don't remember it.
Not there when I passed by this morning.
Or any morning before
Before
Never there
Never blue nor red
Never purple nor yellow.
Never.
Never seen against the emerald green
Illuminated in the noonday sun
spotlighted
highlighted
There.
Never glimpsed in the dark on a rainy night.
Trimmed neat and low, grass never overgrows
Until the bridge is knocked down and the road detours.
Town proper no longer the destination for those lanes.
Just emptiness and regret beyond.
Trimmer gone and reasons forgotten.
Rust and rot with no tie to bind.
Still I don't remember them there,
those four crosses.

Stark white with black letters,
letters that spell names.
Names lovingly picked
lovingly spoken
loving mourned.
Lovingly.
Grass whole and lush just before the bridge
Always there
Always there
Now pocked,
marred
Adorned with whites and blues and reds and purple
and yellow, just like the sun.

Pink Nails

Beautiful looking
deeper rotten shell of lies
conniving sweetly

Repeat

Hot
Sour
passion pink
lover's kink
but blind eye turned so I can't see
can't feel
can't think.
They stand on the edge
blurred and dark
shadowy and staid
even as the cries come
the bargains and barters
the offers bathed in blood.
Sink ye into the dark, they whisper
and succumb most do, sedate and resolute
but claw to bring welts and tissue under the skin go others
as I
as I
borne of blood yet be
until drained and gray
to force them to kiss the mottled flesh.

Catch 22

Magic clouds
circle the earth
protecting us from
impurities.
As progress abounds
we break down
our semi-porous
immunity.

Façade

Dark.
Light.

Shades.

Never the same
but
always so.
Different sizes,
shapes,
rhymes,

reasons...

yet typed.

A budding rose in a dark hand.

Beautiful?

Yes...

BUT NO.

Sleeping Light

I saw you last night
over by my closet
where you always came to me
when I was young and had no inhibitions.

I saw your brilliant blue
sparkling brightly but subtly,
almost airily.

Your face was faint.
I saw grain and texture
within your chest.
You smiled at me.

Last we talked
I told you my news.
The new happenings and
excitement I told of a life watched.
To cold, frost-covered grass
I spoke my happiness
with no response.
I came to you.
Do I look the same?

Last I remember we sat
and talked my kid talk.
Gibberish that amounted
to not much more than
elation over a cartoon
episode.
Snuggled in your warmth,
I remember that you
talked the talk with me,
laughing jovially at my innocence.

Last I saw was you
half-sized
in brilliant sparkling
blue-
but not you.

I thought I saw you
last night.
Smiling that smile
that used to warm me
when nothing else could.
That warms me now from
within.
You were wearing your
brilliant, sparkling
blue.

The Silence of Morning

I awoke today
in search of my love
no warmth did I feel
from the arm that held me.
No love did I see
in the eyes that used to caress me.

I'll search the heavens
and this cold earth
for my one love.
To make him warm
within my soul is my desire.
To keep him whole and safe
I crave deep within my loins.

Where are you, my love?
I fear you've gone
beyond my reach.
I cry at your feet.

Storm Warning

I see a storm in the distance.
I can feel its rumble beneath the surface.
The clouds are darkening over the land in patches.
The air is thin.

I see a storm in the distance.
Rains that will wash away the constant stream of blood
that runs rampant from our mother's womb
as she hangs her worn head.

I see a storm in the distance.
One that will manifest a fire so hot
it will disintegrate all in its path...
...in an instant...
...with no forgiveness.

I see a storm in the distance.
And it will encompass the earth
beating heavy upon our beings and,
in its wake, will reveal a utopia
unparalleled...
for some.

Bad News

I saw him standing there
poise slightly mistook.
Stay away, my head tells me
but my heart beckons me look.

Temptation and Consequence

It's there
looming overhead
discretely
but blatantly

It does not move
rather mills atop
prepared
with its hind-legs
smooth and long
humming a sweet,
treacherous song

To Hesitate

Brick.
Reddish brown, like burnt umber
Red like fall leaves
red
dead
on the ground
trampled underfoot.

Brick.
Brick that speaks of blood
That speaks of pain
That tells of Fortunato's folly.

Mortar
White, not gray
White
bright
blinding
glowing as the day turns,
as the wind shifts,
as the
sun hides behind the clouds
afraid to show,
afraid to see.

White, not gray
gray as it should be
gray as pallid skin
gray as ashes that blow in the wind
to mingle with the leaves.

Under the Blue Moon

Night falls, orange burning from the center to fry the moon
too soon
too soon.
All tuned is my scythe, my sickle quite nice
oiled and ready to cut
to prune.
But mind's eye can see
me
me
not ready.

As the moon turns blue, I wonder after eyes that no longer see
skin turned gray in the haze
after the flay.
Taygeta bites at Maia
dead upon the dead
strange cannibalism in the sky
so bright
too bright
blinding in its brutality
as particles, like so much flesh, fly.
Work to do
blades to lick clean of the blood they let
still I stand watching the flame turn to black
engulfing the sky in ash
blue moon turning skin blue black.

Scattered brain
scattered me.
Come ge' we?
Don't you agree?
It's scary…
Talons, bloody and dirty, all up in my tea.

Si.

Because I do.
I see and know and understand and confirm.
Sasquatch and prophets
Samson holding his hair in his tattooed hand
bloody scalp be damned.

And the cabal says, "Amen!"

I see.
They're in need.
Dying
living
the blade they seek.
Cold metal thrums in response
Hot with want
Orange me.

So, oui.

I come
para ti.

Do This

When the days are long
Speak spells to keep the beasts back
Eyes closed, fingers bent
Bloody hands, scrapped knees give true
All to sate the fickle's mood.

What Voice Does Speak

It calls to me
The dark
From the shadows of cast by rotted eaves
Or with the voice of the wind.

It calls to me
Beckons me forth
To greet it with open arms
Cracked and chafed from nightly encounters of
Its hateful whims.

It calls to me
Softly at times
Like a mother might a child.
Like a lover would another,
Of which it is mine.
Then loudly
Mockingly
Painfully divine.

It calls every night
Its only desire that I not see the evil beauty of my love,
the beast controlling me.

Food for Thought

Trees.
Sky.
Sun.
Moon.
Land.
Water.
Air.
Food.

End soon?

Hell

Darkness thick as tar
unyielding
surrounding me with fear.

Lost memories float above
Teasing me with the remnants
of times past
when I was happy
when I was whole.

Those times seem long gone and distant
even though I can taste your lips
like jasmine.
My mind cries out in pain
as I touch your blackness
and curve you in my dark

and turn my head in shame.

My Darkest Hour

My darkest hour
shone brightly in the sun
to me, 'twas gray,
overcast and solemn
as I felt my lowest
and stood at my blackest.

The warm day and pleasant breeze
beat my skin mercilessly
as the glare blinded my sight.
Black and White for me
yellows and oranges for the world
as White hands on Black arms
did drag.

My darkest hour descended on me
like death
like departure
like sin
while laughter and joy filled the air
deafening me with shame.

The beginning of summer they relished
and mistook my open-mouthed cries for glee
as I watched the play
unravel before me.

In The Distance

Through the glare of the sun
I saw you standing
alone
waiting.

How clearly I saw your face
in my mind
for you have left me
and all
behind.

Through the haze of the sweltering sun
I saw you
smiling
in the distance
at me.

How brilliant and full your smile
was
then
when you smiled at me
from eternity.

Night Visitor

By the light of the moon
It comes to me
Traipsing lightly on air
just above the ground
invisible to all
but to me, I see

Over outstretched lands
he travels to me
in the dead of night
to light my dreams
or my reality

Differently it loves
from times past
he brings happiness
that today will never see

Hot Summer Day

Long summer
come to an end
'tis when my sorrow
do begin

I seen 'im out
in the street
ain't e'en tryin'
to be discrete

Hot summer musta caught 'im
when he saw her sexy brown
always up on her
when she come to town
but now he cain't catch her
'cause she won't never come 'round

Cool an' still
her body do lay
after I met her in the park
yesterday

She gone now, for good
but in this new day
I's gone too
'cause they takin' me away

My Place

The water envelops me
circling me in its warmth,
teasing me with its wave
imagined.

I listen to the silence
and see the crayon sun
shining above my head.
Casting a brilliant light
on all it touches
in my porcelain shell.

Life

I passed the dregs of down
quickly
running through the
adversities that held some
by the legs as they
lunged
toward my existence.

I turned to help
but they were stone,
as Lot's wife a
pillar of salt.

Through down
quickly I ran
chin to chest
hand outstretched
warding off pain
and suffering
fall at my feet.

Full Circle

I look down upon the hunter green fields of night
and see
Towards fields of sorrow
my love runs
Away, said he,
my journey calls
I bid thee farewell

Evermore, I asked
needing to know
why

My darling, what speak you,
a voice
his voice
yet not
asked thunderously,
for I have not gone

I look out my window,
suddenly compelled by
the hot summer streets below
and all there is to see

Full of life
yet dead with loss
(away your being)
cops chasing
glass breaking
sweaty bodies form a
barrier of eager,
interested
exploitative eyes
quest not flesh, but poison get

at the lifeless form
at one with the earth

Evermore, said he.

The Wall

Hard as stone
cold and dark.
Its ominous structure
talks to me harshly,
barking incongruent
insults, confidently
excoriating me for
imagined wrong doings
as if I were meant
to understand.

Rough
jagged edges jut out
at me
piercing my skin
but they leave no scar.

Invisible hands grab me
and pull me into its
redoubtable darkness.
I shrink underneath
its strength
mentally rebelling but
unable to verbally protest.

Stark, dim fissures
like eyes stare stoically
through me seeing my soul
and being disgusted
with it.

I pound my fists
relentlessly against
its austere surface

until they are bloody,
as bloody as my face
from the blow of the wind.

The Dark

Peering into the darkness
I have a sense of one
with me
searching also
for themselves
but finding me.

Voices in the Wind

Sometimes when I walk
I hear voices.

I turn my head but I am alone.
Just me and the wind.

Are you there?
I can feel your touch on my skin.
It burns under the warmth.
It stings.

Dust and grit flying in the wind as it whirls around me
at top speed.
Are you there?

I can hear you.
The sound is faint, but ever so clear.
You call my name.

No.

The wind howls in despair.

Suffocating.
I can't catch my breath.
Life in movement surrounding me
as I watch mine float away.

I fall.
I stand.

I shake.
I am still...here.

Are you there?

Still

Still
Skin toughened by the elements, the sentiments, the precedence
to form armor that protects

Still
Impenetrable, imagined so, but the air finds its weakness and
pushes its poison slow

Still
In the room, in the womb, bespoke doom even though painted
smiles bid hello and goodbye unseen

What the Water Brings

I close my eyes to sink
to fall
to succumb
mouth filling
metallic brine
as I transform.
From the shore they watch but don't see
can't see
because it isn't me they look for
call for
shriek for as their knees weaken
and give way to the weight on their shoulders from the bodies
they bore
the bodies they paid nevermind.
It isn't me who will emerge to lift them
hold them
encircle their throats with an icy hand
leaving a trail of weed in its wake.
Not me
the me they want
the me they expect
but me evermore.
Through bloodshot eyes and gaping mouth I change
I see
I be
who I am
naturally
and they cower
they scream
when they see.
The water lifts me above their heads
my feet at their chests hoisted by the foam
majestically
eternally

unmistakably
and they stare reverently
at
Me.

Society

That sound traveled fast.
His agony on display.
We stood and watched death.

ABOUT THE AUTHOR

L. Marie Wood is an award-winning psychological horror author and screenwriter. She won the Golden Stake Award for her novel *The Promise Keeper* and Best Horror, Best Short, and Best Afrofuturism/Horror/Sci-Fi screenplay awards at several film festivals. An Active member of the HWA, Wood's short fiction has been published in *Slay: Stories of the Vampire Noire* and the Bram Stoker Finalist anthology, *Sycorax's Daughters*. Learn more about her at www.lmariewood.com or join the discussion on Twitter at @LMarieWood1 or on Facebook at www.facebook.com/LMarieWood.

ALSO BY L. MARIE WOOD

For Falstaff Books

The Lost Stories

Imitation of Life

At Mocha Memoirs

Telecommuting

The Black Hole

About Horror: The Study and The Craft

At Cedar Grove Publishing

Affinity Saga, Book One: The Tryst

Mars, the Band Man, and Sara Sue

The Promise Keeper

Crescendo

The Realm Trilogy

The Realm, Book 1

Cacophony, The Realm Book 2

Accursed, The Realm Book 3

FRIENDS OF FALSTAFF